New Girl in Town

New Girl in Town

Anne Harler

Cover photo by
The Photographic Illustrators

Published by Willowisp Press, Inc.
401 E. Wilson Bridge Road, Worthington, Ohio 43085

Printed in the United States of America
10 9 8 7 6 5 4 3 2 1

ISBN 0-87406-218-7

One

JENNIFER Barnes hurried down the hall to her locker and opened it. Then she quickly jammed her sweater and gym clothes inside. She had five minutes until the late bell rang. It was just enough time to find Karla and tell her the great news.

Karla was standing by her open locker, combing her tangled mop of curly brown hair.

"Just look at this mess," she said as Jennifer hurried up to her.

"You look great, honest," Jennifer said, breathlessly. "Guess what?"

"She's coming, isn't she?" Karla said excitedly. "Your cousin is actually moving down here from Chicago!"

"Yes." Jennifer still couldn't believe it herself. "Dawn and Aunt Grace will be here this Thursday."

"Wow, that's really fast." Karla's large

brown eyes grew even larger. "What's she going to think of a small town like this after living in the big city? She'll probably be bored out of her mind, especially with all she's done."

"I know." Jennifer nodded as she glanced into the mirror hanging on Karla's locker door. She wished she could make her freckles disappear and swap her nose for a straighter one. Her semi-curly hair was okay, though she wished it was blonder like it was when she was younger. Now it was an inbetween color—not quite blond but not really brown either.

"Are Dawn and her mom going to stay with you?" Karla asked, glossing her lips while she talked.

"No, Mom and Dad found this furnished apartment for them not far from our house." She sighed. "I hope Dawn won't be too upset by the change."

"It's too bad that Dawn's parents separated," Karla said.

"I know." Jennifer nodded. "Mom said Aunt Grace is pretty broken up about it."

"I bet Dawn is too." Karla slammed her locker door shut and they headed for homeroom. "I know I would be if my dad left us."

"Me, too." Jennifer could almost feel the painful thought slice through her. "So Mom says I have to help Dawn all I can. You know, help her get acquainted at school and show her around. Maybe we can get her a date for the Harvest Hop."

"I'll help," Karla said. "In fact, I can't wait to meet her. She sounds so grown up. She's sure had a lot of experiences for an eighth grader."

"A lot more than I have, that's for sure." Jennifer swung her purse by its long strap as they walked down the hall.

"Well, Dawn's had a lot more chances to do stuff like modeling in fashion shows and being on TV in Chicago than we have in Galesburg," Karla said.

"It doesn't hurt that she's so good-looking," Jennifer added.

"It's too bad it doesn't run in the family," Karla laughed, giving Jennifer a poke in the ribs.

Jennifer laughed at Karla's joke as they paused at the door to homeroom. "She even gets to stay out until eleven o'clock on dates," she said. "Mom says I have to wait until I'm fifteen, if anybody ever asks me."

"Eleven o'clock?" Karla did a great imitation of someone about to faint. "Give me air."

"I'm sure Dawn will look great for my party," Jennifer said. Then she grinned,

7

waiting for Karla's reaction.

"What party?" Karla yelled. She jumped as the late bell rang.

"The one I'm giving for Dawn on Saturday night." Jennifer kept an eye on Mrs. Lewis, their homeroom teacher. "You're invited."

"Great. I can't wait." Karla pulled on her long green sweater so that it covered her hips. "Only . . . ."

"Only what?" Jennifer asked, watching Mrs. Lewis walk slowly toward them.

"Only I just hope you won't spend so much time with her that you won't have any time, well, that we won't get to spend as much time together."

"Don't be silly," Jennifer said. "Cousin or no cousin, you'll always be my very best friend. You know that no one will ever come between us. Not even a boy."

Karla smiled and Jennifer smiled back. They'd been best friends since second grade. Jennifer couldn't imagine a day going by without talking to Karla.

"Girls, come inside and take your seats," Mrs. Lewis said. "Whatever you're talking about now can wait until homeroom period is over."

But Jennifer wondered about that. She had a surprise planned for Dawn's party and she

8

was bursting to tell Karla. It would be agony to wait even twenty seconds.

Dawn and Aunt Grace arrived on Thursday afternoon. Jennifer watched their car, piled high with suitcases and boxes, pull into the driveway of the apartment house down the street. Aunt Grace had decided to close their apartment in Chicago for now and move all their furniture later, when they were settled more permanently.

By Saturday afternoon they were nearly unpacked. When Dawn heard about the party, she told Jennifer she'd try to come early and help.

"This is going to be so much fun," Jennifer said as she and her mother filled plates with cookies and brownies on Saturday evening. "Imagine, having a cousin who's a celebrity."

"You're sweet to introduce her to your friends right away," her mom said. "You know that we're Grace and Dawn's only relatives so they really appreciate all our help just now," Mrs. Barnes went on.

Jennifer giggled as she broke open a sack of potato chips and emptied it into a dish. "It's hard to imagine Dad as someone's baby brother. I wonder if Aunt Grace will have all kinds of stories to tell on him."

"Mind your own business, young lady."

Jennifer's mom tried to look solemn, but her sparkly green eyes gave her away. "You might get in trouble with your dad."

The doorbell rang and Jennifer ran to answer it. Karla and Sue Beth stood in the open doorway.

"Are we the first to get here?" Karla asked, coming in and throwing her jacket on a chair.

"Yep. Come into the kitchen and help me open some root beers."

"Did you invite any boys?" Sue Beth asked, smoothing her long, blond hair with her fingers.

"Not exactly," Jennifer said. "But can I help it if they drop in just when I'm having a party?"

"Jen, I can't believe you actually did it," Karla said just before she stuffed a cookie in her mouth.

"Matt told me you'd asked him," Sue Beth put in, eyeing the brownies thoughtfully. "And he said he'd walk me home tonight. I think he's going to ask me to the Harvest Hop." She paced nervously back and forth between the table and sink. "He's been hinting since school started. I wonder if I can lose five pounds by then."

"If I can ever get Robbie to talk, maybe he'll ask me," Karla said.

"At least you both have your eyes on somebody," Jennifer said. "I don't even have any prospects."

"Where's Dawn?" Karla asked, snatching a potato chip. "Is she upstairs talking to your folks?"

Jennifer shook her head as she walked into the living room. The other girls followed. The doorbell was ringing again.

"Maybe that's Dawn now," Sue Beth said, running to the front window.

But it was several more friends from school. Jennifer was beginning to feel disappointed. Dawn had said she would be early, but now she was already late.

"Let's listen to some music," she said. Jennifer put her newest tape in her player but she knew that her friends were only half listening. She knew they were waiting for Dawn's arrival.

"I can't wait to meet her," Sue Beth said. "I'll bet she's thin, like all models are."

"She's . . . she's just right." Jennifer didn't want to talk about Dawn's thin figure when Sue Beth was trying to lose weight. Sue Beth wasn't really fat, but she always seemed to think of herself that way.

"I just know I saw Dawn on television." Karla ran her fingers through her hair while

11

she talked. "I'm so excited about meeting her."

"Me, too!" Sue Beth added. "I've never met a real celebrity before."

"She's only my cousin," Jennifer said. But she felt a little nervous too. Dawn wasn't anything like her friends in Galesburg.

They listened to Jennifer's new tape twice on both sides before Dawn finally came.

"Sorry, I'm late." She rushed in, breathless and smiling.

Jennifer thought that Dawn looked gorgeous in her blue pants and shirt worn under a bright yellow jacket. Her black hair came just to her shoulders and flipped under in a bouncy style. Her sky-blue eyes were set off by the longest eyelashes Jennifer had ever seen. Are they real? Jennifer wondered to herself, or does Dawn use a curler to make them look longer? Jennifer decided to ask her when she got to know her better.

Jennifer started to introduce Dawn to her friends, but before she knew it they had all begun introducing themselves and chatting noisily.

"There's tons of food in the dining room," Jennifer yelled, over the noise. "Mom says you have to eat all of it before you can go home tonight."

Everyone laughed and headed for the table.

"This is a great party!" Dawn said. "Thanks for having it, Jennifer. Now it won't be so lonesome at school on Monday. At least I'll know a few girls."

"Maybe you'll know a few boys too," Sue Beth said. "When are they crashing the party, Jen?"

"You mean, boys are coming?" Dawn asked. She flipped her hair away from her shoulders in a quick, studied movement.

"Uh-huh." Sue Beth smoothed her pink sweater over her waist. "Jennifer put the word out."

"I wish you would have told me," Dawn said. "I would have worn something different." Dangly, silver earrings swung against her neck.

"Sorry," Jennifer said. "I should have. I mean, you are the guest of honor and everything."

"Maybe I should comb my hair," Dawn said.

"You look great," Karla said. "The guys will love you just the way you are."

"Wait till you meet my boyfriend, Matt," Sue Beth said. "He pitches for the school baseball team."

Now Jennifer began to worry that Matt and Robbie and the other guys wouldn't come. Her party was dying. All of a sudden, the girls seemed self-conscious around Dawn. You'd think that Dawn was a movie star or something, the way everyone was acting, Jennifer thought.

Sue Beth gave a sudden shriek. "I saw them, they're coming up the walk." She ran to the front door and opened it. Karla and some of the other girls joined Sue Beth.

"Come on, Dawn," Jennifer said. "Don't you want to meet some guys from our class?"

"They look so young and immature," she said under her breath as she walked to the door with Jennifer.

"Hey, you guys," Jennifer said to the new arrivals. "This is my cousin from Chicago, Dawn Brewer."

"I'm pleased to meet all of you," Dawn said, shaking each boy's hand as she was introduced. When she was introduced to Matt Dorsey, she said, "I'll bet you play baseball. Are you a pitcher?"

Matt's eyes widened. "Yeah, how did you know?"

"You look so strong," Dawn said. "Would you like something to eat?" She took his arm and they headed for the dining room.

"She doesn't waste much time," Karla whispered to Jennifer as the other kids trailed along after Matt and Dawn.

"Yeah," Sue Beth said miserably. "He never even noticed me."

"He's just being polite to the new girl in town," Jennifer said. "Come on, let's put some records on so we can dance. Why don't you ask Matt to help?"

But Sue Beth didn't have a chance, Jennifer noticed. The moment Dawn heard the music she began to dance with Matt. Soon other kids were dancing as well.

Finally Jennifer could relax a little. The party seemed to be moving now and Dawn sure was doing her part to make it work. Everyone was having a good time, eating, dancing, and talking.

Everyone but Sue Beth. She sat on the sofa staring at Matt who was doing a good job of staring at Dawn. He seemed to be lapping up the attention Dawn was giving him.

Why did she have to single Matt out? Jennifer thought to herself. Hadn't she heard Sue Beth say that Matt was her boyfriend? Jennifer hated to think that Dawn had heard and didn't care.

The party ended at 9:30 and most of the kids left. Only Karla and Dawn stayed.

"Thanks for the great time," Dawn said, putting on her bright yellow jacket and heading for the front door. "It was a great way to begin my new life in Galesburg."

"Don't you want me to walk you home?" Jennifer asked.

"No, thanks. Matt's waiting outside." Dawn flipped her hair back. "He wants to make sure I don't get lost on my first night." She winked as she closed the front door.

Karla and Jennifer stood quietly for a moment, not speaking, not moving. They both just stared at the closed door.

Then Karla said softly, "Wow, she knows all the right moves, doesn't she?" Karla paused. "I wonder if she gives lessons?"

Two

"WHAT time do we get out of school today?" Dawn asked Jennifer as they walked to school on Monday morning.

"Three o'clock," Jennifer answered, looking down the street for Karla. "Why?"

"I thought it would be fun to go roller skating," Dawn said. "Dad gave me new skates just before he . . . just before he left. Is there a rink around here?"

"There's one downtown."

"Good." Dawn smiled. "If we go right to the rink from school, we can get in two or three hours before dinner."

Jennifer frowned. Karla was late today. "I don't know if I can do that," she said. "I'll have to go home and ask Mom first."

"Jen, you're in eighth grade. Aren't you a little old to have to run and ask your mom everything? Can't you call her from school?"

"I guess so." Jennifer paused, wondering why it was so important to hurry to the rink from school. "Why don't we ask some of the other girls, like Karla?"

"I'd rather not," Dawn said. "I'd like to go with just you, Jennifer. I really want to get to know my one and only cousin." Then she linked her arm through Jennifer's. "I hope we get to be best friends."

Jennifer smiled uneasily. I've got a best friend, she thought. Then she rememberd how tough things were for Dawn and Aunt Grace. "We'll have lots of fun together," she promised.

Ten minutes later, they were hurrying across the junior high campus and into the main building.

"The office is down this hall," Jennifer said. "You'll need to register and pick up your schedule. Oh, there's Sue Beth."

Then Jennifer wished she hadn't said that. Dawn would probably be embarrassed to speak to Sue Beth after the way she'd acted with Matt on Saturday night. And Sue Beth probably wouldn't be thrilled to see Dawn again either.

"Hi, Sue Beth," Dawn called. "How are you?"

Sue Beth turned to look at them. A smile

appeared for a second on her face. Then it quickly disappeared. She hurried down the hall, away from them.

"Well, aren't we friendly," Dawn said. "What's wrong with her? Is she moody or something?"

"No, Sue Beth is the easiest person in the world to be around," Jennifer answered.

"She's sure not acting it."

Jennifer wondered how Dawn would act if the girl who stole her boyfriend tried to act as if it never happened? Instead, she said aloud, "The office is right here. See you later." Then she ran after Sue Beth.

She caught up with her near the music room. "Sue Beth, I'm sorry about what happened Saturday night."

"It's not your fault," Sue Beth said. "And I should be as mad at Matt as I am at her. I just don't understand how she can act as if nothing happened."

"Me, either." Jennifer shook her head. "But I'll try to talk to her. I really will."

"Thanks, Jen. You're a good friend." Shifting her book bag to her other arm, Sue Beth hurried into her homeroom.

I can talk to Dawn about Sue Beth and Matt this afternoon when we're skating, Jennifer resolved. Now I've got to find Karla and tell her I can't go over to her house after school.

Jennifer waited by Karla's locker until the tardy bell rang, but Karla didn't show up. At lunchtime she called her mom and got permission to go skating with Dawn.

"But why isn't she going home to get her new skates?" her mom had asked.

Jennifer couldn't answer that, even though she'd wondered about it too.

"By the way, Karla phoned," her mom said. "She said to tell you she's sick with a cold but she can still talk on the phone."

Jennifer laughed. "She can do that in her sleep."

As soon as the final bell rang that afternoon, Dawn and Jennifer caught the first bus and rode downtown to the skating rink.

"Isn't this more fun than going straight home?" Dawn asked. "I was afraid Galesburg was going to be boring, so I decided to do something about it. I'm having lots of fun."

"Good." Jennifer looked at Dawn's eyes through her long curly eyelashes. "I'm glad everything's better than you expected. How does your mom feel about things?"

"Not that great." Dawn pulled a mirror from her purse and looked at herself. "She spends a lot of time moping around."

"I can understand why," Jennifer said.

"She can't let it get to her, that's all."
Dawn's eyes looked glittery, as if she might
cry. "She's got to get out of the house and
start having fun like me."

"Maybe you ought to tell her that."

"Mom and I don't talk much about things.
In fact, we don't talk much at all." Dawn
leaned back in her seat and didn't say anything for a while. Then she added, "But I
could talk to Dad. Any time."

The moment they stepped inside Jennifer
understood why Dawn had been in such a
hurry to get to the rink.

"Hi, Matt," Dawn called.

Matt had been talking to a group of boys.
He whirled around when he heard his name.

"Hi, Dawn." He looked happy to see her.
"Why didn't you tell me you were coming
here?"

"I didn't know it myself." Dawn linked her
arm through Jennifer's. "But my fantastic
cousin decided to show me all the fun places
in Galesburg. This must be one of them,
especially if you're here."

"Why aren't you at baseball practice?"
Jennifer asked Matt stiffly.

Matt tore his eyes away from Dawn for a
second. "Baseball practice doesn't start until
spring, remember? That's when we play it."

Then he turned to look at Dawn again.

Jennifer felt her face go hot. Of course—baseball was a spring and summer game. The only people who played it during October were the pros in the World Series.

"Do you need skates?" Matt was saying to Dawn. "The rentals aren't that bad here. Come on."

"Oh, thanks, Matt," Dawn said. "I can use your help, especially when I try to stand on them." She walked away with Matt to the rental room.

Now what was that all about? Jennifer wondered. She's skated for half of her life. Why is she pretending she doesn't know how?

"Hi, Jennifer."

She turned around. "Oh, hi, Peter."

Peter Walton looked as if he was ready to blush. Jennifer could see the redness starting to appear underneath his freckles. He sure seems to blush a lot around me, Jennifer thought to herself. But maybe he did that around all the girls he talked to.

"Peter, I didn't know you skated. I mean, I thought you studied all the time." Whoops, that didn't sound right. She was making him sound like the brain of the week.

"Most of the time I do." He brushed back a pile of strawberry-blond hair that was always falling in his serious blue eyes. "But Matt and some of the guys dared me that I couldn't stand up on these things and I don't know what got into me." He looked at the skates in his hands as if they'd attack any second. "I'll probably fall on my face though. I'm not very athletic."

Poor Peter, Jennifer thought. He can tell you the answer to the world's most complicated math problems, but he's afraid to roller skate. "Hey, Pete, I'm pretty good in this subject. If you promise to help me with math, I'll teach you how to skate."

"Will you really?" His eyes looked brighter. "It's a deal."

Besides, Jennifer thought, as she led him to the rink moments later. I've got nothing else to do until Dawn decides to go home. Might as well teach the brain of the school one thing he doesn't know how to do.

Peter only fell twice the first time around the rink, but he'd never have gotten up if Jennifer hadn't been there. He acted as if his bones had turned to rubber bands when he tried to stand. She wondered if he danced the way he skated.

"You're not coordinated," Jennifer said, trying not to laugh as she grabbed Peter's elbow again. "But you sure are brave."

"Or dumb," Peter said, grabbing her arm and leaning hard. "How did I let myself get talked into this?"

Jennifer noticed, when she glanced at the the other guys, that they weren't watching Peter anyway. If they had done this for a laugh, they'd forgotten about it. They were too busy watching Dawn skate with Matt.

At first Matt put his arm around Dawn's waist. Then he guided her carefully around the rink. Gradually she skated better and better. Soon she was doing little whirlies and even skating backward. If Matt believed she was a beginner, then he really was goofy-brained.

"Why don't we stop a minute?" Peter asked, grasping the rail. "I don't want to wear you out."

"Sounds good." Jennifer led the way to the exit and sat down on a bench. Peter collapsed beside her. "You're really doing okay," she said. "You shouldn't expect too much the first time."

"I didn't know it would be this hard," he said, wiping his face with the sleeve of his knit shirt. Then he glanced up. "Who's that girl with Matt?"

"My cousin Dawn from Chicago," Jennifer said.

"She's beautiful." Peter started to lightly

blush again. "Where did she learn to skate like that?"

"She took lessons," Jennifer said. "She's taken lessons in a lot of things." Especially in boys, she added to herself.

Jennifer watched as Robbie Hendriks came out to skate with Dawn. Robbie had been hanging around Karla's locker a lot lately and Karla seemed pretty interested in him. Jennifer wondered if Karla knew what a great skater Robbie was or if he'd been keeping that to himself. He sure wasn't keeping it a secret from Dawn, Jennifer thought.

Matt came off the rink to watch Dawn and Robbie. "Where did she learn to skate like that?" he asked.

"Why don't you ask her?" Jennifer said.

"Maybe I will," Matt said glumly.

Maybe he knows how Sue Beth felt at my house last Saturday night, Jennifer thought.

She left the rink at 5:30 after promising to give Peter another lesson soon. Dawn decided to stay a while longer. She was still skating when Jennifer walked out the door. One of the guys would ride the bus home with Dawn. In fact, she couldn't figure out why Dawn had wanted her to come in the first place.

"Is that you, hon?" her mom called from the kitchen when Jennifer walked in the door.

"No, it's the Queen of England."

"Well, Your Majesty, I hope you'll tell your friend Karla to find some other form of amusement. She has telephoned five times, wanting to know if you're home yet," she said. Her mom came in and gave her a hug with floury hands.

Jennifer smiled as she dialed Karla's number. Karla answered the phone on the first ring.

"So what's up?" Jennifer asked.

"Where were you?" Karla's voice sounded nasal. "Here I sit, sick and lonely. Never mind, don't tell me. I've got news first. I saw this ad in the paper this morning."

"What ad?"

"About a photo contest that Ryan's Youth Shop is having. Since you weren't home I did it without you."

"Did what?"

"Entered us in the Fashion Friend Photo Contest, that's what," Karla said.

"What's that?" Jennifer sank to the floor. This was going to be one of Karla's marathon talks she could tell. She might as well get comfortable.

"Well, it works this way. You and a friend look for clothes in your closets that you think will go well together. Like, you're going to a school play or football game or slumber party."

"You mean, we dress as if we're going some special place together."

"You got it. Of course, if we can't find stuff in our own closets, the store would love to have us buy new outfits from them."

"That figures." Jennifer pulled off her shoes and wiggled her toes. "So now we've got our clothes. Then what?"

"Someone takes our pictures modeling them. The best picture wins."

"Wins what?"

"New clothes from the store and a chance to model in their style show in December."

"That sounds like fun. Let's do it."

"I already did. I sent in our application today. Now tell me what's been going on." Karla sneezed right after she finished talking.

Then Jennifer told Karla about skating with Dawn, but left out the part about Robbie. It sounded better that way.

Three

"**O**KAY, we'll see you at six o'clock," Jennifer heard her mom say into the phone after school.

"Hi, Mom," Jennifer said as soon as her mom hung up. "Who was that on the phone?"

"Aunt Grace," Mrs. Barnes answered. "The weather has turned so warm that I thought we ought to have one more cook-out before cold weather comes. Grace and Dawn are joining us."

"It's really Indian summer, all right." Jennifer looked out the window above the sink. Gold, yellow, green, and crimson were everywhere.

"If you've nothing better to do, you can peel potatoes," her mother's voice interrupted her thoughts.

"I just remembered, I have to call Karla. Then I'll come and peel."

"Bet you haven't talked to her for at least five minutes. Not since you said good-bye on your special corner," Jennifer's mom teased.

"I have to stay informed, don't I?" Jennifer laughed as she hurried upstairs to the hall telephone. Ordinarily she and Karla would have talked on the way home. But now that Dawn was walking with them, their talks and walks weren't the same. Instead, she and Karla saved things to talk about until later, when they could be alone.

Karla answered on the second ring. "I didn't say anything about the photo contest," she began without saying hello.

"I noticed." Somehow they decided, without even talking about it, they wouldn't tell Dawn about the contest. But Jennifer didn't feel right about it. It was as if she didn't trust her very own cousin.

"When can you come over?" Karla was saying. "We need to practice putting on makeup. And we have to pick out which clothes we'll wear for the picture."

Jennifer thought. "How about tomorrow?"

"Tomorrow?" Karla's voice rose. "How about tonight? We have to start deciding on things pretty soon. Are you sure you want to do this?"

"We're having company tonight," Jennifer

interrupted. "So I have to stay home."

"Who's coming?" Karla asked, sounding disappointed. She paused, then went on. "Don't tell me, it's Dawn and her mom."

"Okay, I won't tell you." There was a long pause. "Well, I guess tomorrow is all right," Karla said. "I have a lot of homework anyway."

"Karla, I'm really sorry." Jennifer didn't know what she was sorry about, but she felt she had to say it anyway. "I'll see you first thing in the morning."

Mr. Barnes arrived home just as Dawn and Aunt Grace were driving up. Soon he was cooking hamburgers on the barbecue and Jennifer's stomach was growling hungrily.

Aunt Grace stood beside Mr. Barnes, looking like a wilted flower. Jennifer remembered her as a classy dresser who loved to wear stylish and brightly colored clothes. She had worked in a dress shop for years. But right now she looked faded. Even her dark eyes looked faded.

Jennifer hurried over to Aunt Grace and gave her a hug. "Don't those hamburgers smell good, Aunt Grace?" she asked. "I could eat a dozen."

"I might be able to eat one," Aunt Grace said. Her pale face had sad lines in it. She looked like she had lost more weight in the week since they'd arrived.

"Here come the baked beans," Mrs. Barnes said, coming out of the back door with a steaming dish in her hands. "And I'll be right back with the potato salad and cole slaw."

"I'll help," Dawn said and hurried inside after Jennifer's mom.

"That's a wonderful daughter you've got there, Grace," Mr. Barnes said, pointing after Dawn with his barbecue fork. "I'm glad she's around to look after you. And she's also a good influence on Jennifer."

"I think she misses her dad more than she says." Aunt Grace's voice sounded quavery. "This has been harder on her than she's letting on."

Jennifer walked over to the picnic table and smoothed out the cloth covering it. Dawn sure hides it, she thought. If she's hurting, she doesn't show it. She's only mentioned her dad a couple of times.

After they'd finished eating, Jennifer's dad, mom, and Aunt Grace sat over their coffee, talking about relatives Jennifer didn't know.

"Can we be excused?" Dawn asked quietly. "I'll bet you grownups have things to talk about that's private."

Mr. Barnes laughed. "As a matter of fact we've got a few relatives you're better off not knowing about. Sure, you girls run along."

Jennifer followed Dawn inside. "Do you want to watch TV?" she asked.

"No, I can watch television at home," Dawn said. "Where's a telephone with a lot of privacy?"

"There's one upstairs in the hall, or in my folks' bedroom."

"That's the one for me." Dawn headed for the stairs. Jennifer started to follow.

"Where are you going?" Dawn demanded.

"I'm just going to show you where the phone is," Jennifer said. "I figured you didn't know."

"Well, okay." Dawn fluffed her bouncy dark hair. "It's just that . . . you know, this is a private call. It's personal."

Dawn followed Jennifer into the master bedroom and sat down on the king-size bed near the telephone. "I met the cutest boy at the skating rink," she said.

"I saw you skating with Robbie," Jennifer answered.

"Not him. Someone else." Dawn looked up, her eyes bright with excitement. "I think this guy goes to high school. Listen, you've got to promise not to tell."

"No problem," Jennifer shrugged. "I'll see you downstairs." She started walking toward the bedroom door.

Dawn grabbed her purse and dumped its contents on the bed. "I know I've got his number here some place."

Jennifer turned around, then stopped as she saw what Dawn had dumped out of her plastic purse. "Where did you get those cigarettes?"

"Not so loud." Dawn quickly stuffed them back in her purse. "I bought them. Where do you think I got them?"

"Why?"

"To smoke, that's why."

"But why smoke?" Jennifer couldn't believe it. She knew a few kids at school did it, but it wasn't something she wanted to do.

"It makes me look older, for one thing," Dawn said, looking at a tattered piece of paper she'd found. "And it's fun to do something you're not supposed to do. Want to try it?"

"No." Jennifer shook her head. "Not me."

The telephone's ring jarred them. Dawn picked up the receiver and handed it to Jennifer.

"Jen, it's me." Karla was speaking excitedly into the phone. "I know you've got company, but I thought you might be able to turn on the TV. There's a program on all about how to do your hair to make you look more sophisticated. We can use that for the contest."

"What channel is it on?"

34

"Channel Eight. See you tomorrow."

"Right."

Dawn was laughing as Jennifer hung up. "Karla doesn't need a telephone. You can hear her talking all the way downtown without one. If you want to watch TV, it's okay. I'll be down in a minute."

"Sounds good," Jennifer said.

Later, when Dawn came downstairs, Jennifer noticed that Dawn's eyes were red. What could that guy have said to make her cry like that? She also wondered what Aunt Grace would do if she knew Dawn was calling older guys and smoking. Jennifer knew she wouldn't tell. Aunt Grace looked unhappy enough already.

Jennifer slept late the next morning. Her dad had already gone off to his health club when she came down for breakfast.

"Have a nice snooze?" her mom asked, sitting down across from her at the table. She was wearing a pink jogging suit with calico rabbits hopping across her chest.

"Real nice." Jennifer looked at her mother's face. Her bright, green eyes were so alive and warm, so different from Aunt Grace's. Jennifer needed to talk about Dawn and the mixed-up feelings she was having for her cousin.

"What's going on in that sleepy head of

yours?" Jennifer's mom asked.

"I've been thinking. . . ."

"That sounds promising."

"No, this is serious, Mom."

"Sorry, honey. It was the wrong time to tease."

"It's about Dawn," Jennifer began.

"Isn't she great?" Mrs. Barnes said. "I'm so impressed with the way she's helping Grace through all their troubles. That's pretty remarkable for a girl who's probably hurting a lot herself. She was very close to her dad."

Jennifer's words stuck in her throat. Maybe she was getting the wrong impression of Dawn. Maybe she was jealous of Dawn's gorgeous face and her easy way of talking to boys?

"What were you going to say, Jen?" her mother asked with a puzzled tone in her voice.

"Oh, it's nothing." Jennifer poured milk on her cereal. "I . . . I think she's nice too. She made an impression on my friends."

As soon as she finished breakfast, Jennifer dressed, then hurried downstairs. "I'm going to Karla's, Mom," she called at the front door.

"I'll walk to the corner with you," Mrs. Barnes said. They stepped outside into the morning sunshine. "I'm going to see if I can get Grace to take a walk with me. It's too beautiful to stay inside."

36

"Tell Dawn hi," Jennifer called when they reached the corner. She continued down Pine Street to Karla's.

"I will," Mrs. Barnes said as she waved and turned at Elm.

I really do like Dawn, Jennifer thought. But why do I have to keep reminding myself that I do? She wondered about that all the way over to Karla's.

Four

"WELL, what do you think?" Karla waited impatiently at her front door as Jennifer stared at her. "Do you think I've captured the real me?"

Jennifer began to laugh. She tried not to, but she couldn't help it. "Karla, what did you do to your hair?"

"I just followed those directions I heard on TV last night."

"But it looks like you've got horns growing all over your head." Jennifer tried to hold her giggles inside because she could see that Karla was beginning to simmer. In a minute she'd boil over.

"I thought it looked okay." Karla ran to the mirror in the front hall and frowned. "Maybe you're right. I've got a few too many horns."

"Where's your brush?" Jennifer asked. "I'll brush it out."

They went into her bedroom. "My brush is on the dresser," Karla said. She flopped on her unmade bed and began to thumb through a fashion magazine.

Jennifer stared at the top of the dresser. "What is all this stuff?"

"Mom said I could borrow some of her old makeup to practice with." Karla threw her magazine on the floor and stood up. "But I decided to wait until you came. Do you want to be first?"

"Not me," Jennifer said. "Let's practice on you. Let's give you a face to go with that hair. How about a far-out in space-face."

"All right. If it's a space-face you want," Karla said, laughing. "How about this?" She outlined her eyes with thick, black liner.

Jennifer fell on the bed, laughing. Karla had to be the craziest person in the world, and also the most fun.

Next Karla put green eyeshadow on her eyelids and round, bright dots of blusher on her cheeks. "How's that?"

"You look like an extraterrestrial!" Jennifer said, wiping tears from her eyes.

"Now it's your turn." Karla came at Jennifer with a lipstick and eyebrow pencil.

"Help," Jennifer yelled, jumping up and down on the bed. Then she stopped. "Hey, did you hear the doorbell?"

"Oh, no," Karla groaned. "You'll have to answer it. I can't go looking like this."

"Where's your mom?"

"She went to the grocery store." Karla gave Jennifer a push. "Go on, maybe it's Robbie. Tell him . . . tell him. . . ."

"I'll tell him you've turned into an alien!" Jennifer said, hurrying down the hall to the front door.

"Hi, Jennifer." Dawn stood in the entry when Jennifer opened the door. "Your mom said you were coming over here and it was okay to come over too." Her dark hair was pulled back on each side this morning and her matching blue shorts and blouse made her eyes especially blue.

"Come in, Dawn," Jennifer said. "We were just practicing with makeup for. . . ." She stopped, remembering that she and Karla had decided not to say anything about the contest. "For fun," she finished.

"Maybe I can help," Dawn said, looking around the living room. "That modeling course I took in Chicago really taught me a lot about cosmetics."

They went into Karla's bedroom. A moment later she hurried in, her face scrubbed and shining. "Oh, hi Dawn," she said. Then she looked pointedly at Jennifer.

Jennifer knew what that look meant. What is SHE doing here?

"Did my mom get your mom out for a walk?" Jennifer asked it carefully, hoping that Karla would understand her mom was responsible for Dawn's arrival.

"Yes." Dawn was standing by the dresser, fingering the jars and tubes of makeup. "They decided to go to a backyard sale. What is all this stuff?"

Karla explained how she'd borrowed her mother's makeup.

"It does look kind of old-fashioned," Dawn said, a small frown appearing between her eyes. "But let's try it anyway. Come on, Jennifer."

Jennifer sat down in front of the dresser mirror. Dawn looked her face over slowly. Finally she said, "First, we have to do something about those freckles."

Then she went to work. When she finished half an hour later, Jennifer looked in the mirror. She had to admit that Dawn had done a great job. Her freckles had disappeared completely and she looked much older.

"You'll for sure get a date for the dance with that face," Karla said. "Now it's my turn. Make me glamorous too, Dawn. Maybe Robbie will finally ask me to the Hop."

"Do you mean Robbie Hendriks?" Dawn asked, applying something that smoothed out Karla's skin.

Oh, no, Jennifer thought. Is she going to go after him too? Isn't Matt enough?

"That's the one," Karla said. "You met him at the party."

"He's in my math class too," Dawn said.

Jennifer sighed. Maybe Dawn would leave him alone, now that she knew Karla was interested in him too.

At school on Monday morning Jennifer walked slowly toward Karla's locker. She hadn't appeared at their special corner and Jennifer finally left without her.

Now she saw Karla flying down the hall and hurried to meet her. "Where were you?" Jennifer asked when Karla stopped at her locker.

"Putting on my face." Karla turned and Jennifer saw that she was wearing eye-liner and skin cover-up. "It took me so long to get it right that Mom had to drive me. What do you think?"

"Looks great and your hair looks a lot better too." Jennifer stared with admiration. "No horns this morning. How did you learn to do it like this?"

"Dawn came over yesterday afternoon to

show me." Karla began to dial her combination. "She is so terrific and wants to help so much I can't believe it."

"You look older, Karla. At least fourteen."

"I hope Robbie likes me this way," she said. "Oh, here he comes."

"I'll leave then so you two can be alone."

"Alone?" Karla giggled, looking around at the kids jostling one another in the hall. "Don't I wish?"

"Hi," Robbie said, his lopsided grin spreading across his face. "Hey, Jen, I've been meaning to tell you that was some party you gave for your cousin. She's really cool."

"Thanks," Jennifer said. "Maybe I'll give a skating party next. Dawn loves to skate. You do too, don't you Rob?" Jennifer knew that was a loaded question but she couldn't keep the words from coming out of her mouth.

"Sounds good if we can get Karla to come." He leaned against her locker.

"I'm not so sure," Karla said. "If I have to stand up on something thin and sharp, count me out."

"This is roller skating we're talking here," Robbie said. "Not ice skating. Hey, what did you do to yourself? You look neat."

Three's a crowd, Jennifer thought. "I'll see you guys later." She walked away, smiling.

44

Now maybe, Robbie will ask Karla to the dance in November, or at least walk her home from school.

At noon Jennifer waited outside the cafeteria door for Karla but Sue Beth arrived first.

"Do you want to eat with us?" Jennifer asked.

"I'd love to," Sue Beth answered. "I'll go in and save us a place." A moment later Karla arrived and they got in the food line.

"Guess what?" Karla whispered. "Robbie hinted, but it was a big hint, that he was going to call me about something special soon. Isn't that fantastic?"

"Oh, Karla, that's great," Jennifer said. "I just know he's going to ask you to the Hop."

"I hope so," Karla said. "I wish you were going too."

Jennifer shrugged. So far there wasn't anyone around who seemed interested in asking her.

"Hi, everybody," Dawn said behind them. "Can I sit with you?"

"Sure," Karla said. "I'm dying to know more about Chicago."

"Sue Beth is saving a place for us." Jennifer hoped she wouldn't mind eating lunch with Dawn.

They made their lunch selections and walked over to the table where she was waiting. Sue Beth said a cold hello to Dawn, and then closed her mouth tightly.

But Dawn didn't seem to notice. She kept glancing around, watching the door. When Matt and Robbie and Peter walked in together, she waved them over.

Karla looked at Jennifer and raised her eyebrows. She kind of wiggled them up and down in the special way she had that meant she was sending messages. And Jennifer knew what Karla was wanting to say. What's Dawn up to now?

The boys came over with loaded trays. "Sit down everybody," Dawn said. "Isn't this fun?" she went on. "Like a party. Say, why don't we have one again soon?" She looked all around the table. "I'd ask you to our place but it's so small. Do you suppose we could go to your house again, Jennifer?"

"I can ask."

"The last one was a real killer," Dawn said. "I love to dance with people who know how to move." She gave Matt a warm smile.

"You're a good dancer yourself," Matt said, blushing.

"I know." Dawn seemed to be full of ideas. "We could go skating together. Why don't we have a skating party?"

"All those in favor," Robbie said, raising his right hand.

"I just knew you'd like that idea." Dawn smiled at him.

When Jennifer dared to glance at Karla again, she was wiggling her eyebrows furiously. Wow, she was really upset about something. Jennifer didn't have to guess. She knew what had Karla steamed up and didn't blame her one little bit. Now Dawn was moving in on Robbie too. What was her problem anyway?

It's a good thing I don't have a boyfriend, Jennifer thought, or Dawn would try to add him to her list.

Five

A week later Jennifer waited impatiently by Karla's locker. Where was that girl anyway? Jennifer wondered. The last bell of the day had rung over fifteen minutes ago. Karla never dawdled after school. Maybe Robbie had finally asked to walk home with her and she had gone.

Sue Beth rounded the corner and walked down the hall toward her. "Hi, Jen," she said. "I bet you'd like to know where Karla is, wouldn't you?"

Jennifer didn't like the way Sue Beth said that. "Have you seen her? Did she stay after class to get help with science?"

"No, she's in the girls' restroom."

"She's not sick again, is she?"

"She wasn't when I saw her." Sue Beth kept walking. "But I have a feeling she's going to be."

Jennifer stared after her. What was that all about? Well, there's one way to find out, she thought, and hurried down the hall.

She opened the restroom door and knew right away what was going on. "Karla," she called as the door to one of the cubicles swung shut. "It's no use hiding in there. I can smell the smoke."

Slowly, the door opened and Karla stood there, a cigarette held awkwardly in one hand. "Dawn said this was fun," she managed to say. Her face was a washed-out green color.

"Where is she?" Jennifer demanded. "I want to talk to her."

Karla pointed to the next cubicle before throwing her cigarette in the john. "I don't feel so good," she said.

Jennifer pounded on the next cubicle door. "Dawn, come out of there right now."

The door opened and Dawn stood there smiling in the midst of blue smoke. "Hi, Jen," she said. "Did you change your mind?"

"No, I didn't." Jennifer was so mad she could feel her face burning. "And I don't know what you think you're doing unless it's getting Karla in a lot of trouble. We aren't allowed to smoke here at Lombard."

Dawn threw her cigarette away and walked out to stare at herself in the mirror. "Oh, Jen, get real. Half the kids I know do it." She fluffed her dark hair away from her face.

"I'm talking to you two." Jennifer looked at Karla who looked as if she wanted to be some place else. "You're my cousin and Karla's my best . . . ."

"Then why won't you let us have a little fun if you like us so much?" Dawn shouted.

Jennifer could see it was pointless to argue any more. "I give up," she said. "I'm going home. And you two had better get out of here before someone comes in and puts you and the smoke together."

She turned and walked out the door just as a couple of girls came in. I hope they won't tell, she thought.

Jennifer walked slowly home, kicking up the fallen leaves on the sidewalk. This was her next favorite time of year, after summer. She loved autumn and its bright colors and the air that smelled of bonfires and the promise of holidays to come.

So why did she feel this way? Disappointed, lonely, as if she'd lost her best friend?

What was the matter with Karla? She'd been acting so different this past week. It wasn't because of Robbie, it was more. It was Dawn and her idea of what was fun and important. Yes, Jennifer was sure of that.

She stopped right there in front of Mrs. Cartright's house. How are you sure? she asked herself. Are you sure it's because of Dawn or are you just plain jealous because Karla is beginning to spend more time with your cousin? Are you sure you're not the one who's acting different?

"Jen, hey Jen, wait." It was a boy's voice.

"Oh, Peter." She tried not to sound disappointed. "I didn't know you lived out this way."

"I don't." Peter's blush was ready to blossom. He brushed back his strawberry-blond hair and cleared his throat two or three times.

"Have you got a cold?" Jennifer asked.

"No, I'm fine." He began to walk along with her as she turned down Pine Street. "I thought, well, I thought I might just walk you home." He finished quickly and breathed a great sigh.

Jennifer glanced quickly at him. His whole face was blushing now. He looked like he'd been out in the sun too long.

"Okay," she said. "I hope you know that I live down at the end of this street. You'll have a long walk home."

"Oh, that's okay," Peter said quickly. "I don't mind. I've been wanting to talk to you since you helped me at the rink a couple of weeks ago."

"I know you don't need any help with your homework," Jennifer said. "It must be something else."

"Kind of," Peter began. "I thought I'd ask you about Dawn."

Oh, no, she thought. Here we go again. Every boy in school is in love with her. "So what do you want to know?"

"Well, the first thing I'd like to know is . . . ." Peter stopped and took a deep breath. "What is Dawn really like? See, I want to interview her for the paper. I'm the editor, in case you didn't know."

"Why don't you talk to Dawn?" Jennifer asked. "Why ask me?"

"So I can get her real background," Peter explained. His serious blue eyes studied her. "I figure that you're pretty average, not like your cousin at all."

"Thanks a lot." Jennifer felt herself get steamed up over that one. She began to walk faster.

"Oh, I didn't mean that the way it sounded," she heard Peter say from behind her. "You're not even average . . . ."

Jennifer stopped at the hedge that bordered her front yard and turned to face Peter. "For a smart guy you sure say a lot of stupid things," she said before starting up the front walk.

"Wait a minute." Peter ran after her and caught up just as she reached the front porch. "Jennifer, I'm really sorry. I'm just so nervous talking to you that I'm getting my words all mixed up."

Nervous, Jennifer thought. He's nervous talking to me? What he means is he's nervous talking about Dawn. "What words did you get mixed up, Peter?"

"I didn't mean you were average. I meant you were ordinary."

"Great. Is that supposed to be better?"

"What I mean is, Dawn is different because she's lived in a big city and done big city things," Peter said, in a rush. "And you've lived in Galesburg all your life. So I thought I'd compare big city schools with small town ones and find out how they differ by talking about you and Dawn and what you do in school." He breathed in a great gulp of air.

"Are you trying to tell me that you want to interview me too?"

"That's right." Now Peter was smiling. "You're really pretty talented."

"I am?"

"Yes. You drew all the posters for our seventh-grade party last year and helped with

54

the science fair this year and you play trombone . . . ."

"That was in sixth-grade band," Jennifer said. "I don't do that any more."

"And you roller skate," Peter finished. "That takes real talent, at least I think it does."

Jennifer began to relax a little. "Okay, I guess you can talk to me for your story in the paper. But it sounds as if you know just about everything there is to know about me. Do you need to talk to me any more?"

"Oh, yes." Peter nodded. "A lot more. How about tomorrow after school." We could go to the . . . the Dairy Dream or somewhere, and have a yogurt shake while we talk."

Wow, Jennifer thought. If I didn't know better, I'd swear he's asking for a date. But this is Peter, the brain. He doesn't date, does he? "I'll see you then," she said.

Peter was still standing by the front porch steps when she went inside and closed the door. For the first time she dared to think about going to the Harvest Hop. It was the biggest event of the fall semester. There'd be a live band and everything.

"Is that you, Jen?" Mrs. Barnes called from the kitchen.

"No, it's the Statue of Liberty." Jennifer

dumped her book bag on the hall table and walked into the kitchen. "Anybody call me?" She looked in the refrigerator and helped herself to a piece of cheese.

"No, Karla hasn't called yet." Mrs. Barnes turned from the counter where she'd been thumbing through a cookbook. "Come to think of it, she hasn't called this week. You two aren't having a fight, are you?"

Jennifer shook her head and avoided looking at her mother. Karla and I aren't having anything, she thought. Maybe, if we were fighting, I'd feel better about what's going on.

"I'm going to do my homework," Jennifer said, going upstairs.

She flopped on her bed, wondering if Karla was home yet. She really wanted to talk to her. She wanted to make sure she wasn't going to smoke again and to ask her when they were going to get ready for the Fashion Friend Photo Contest. The deadline must be coming up soon. Maybe she's already entered with someone else, Jennifer thought suddenly.

Outside her bedroom, the telephone in the hall began to ring. "I'll get it," Jennifer called, leaping from her bed and running across the room.

"Karla," she yelled into the telephone. "Karla . . . ."

"This is Dawn" she said. "I want to talk to you about . . . you know. Where's your mom?"

Disappointment knotted in Jennifer's stomach. "Mom doesn't listen in on my phone conversations," she said. "What do you want to talk about?"

"Don't be dense," Dawn snapped. "I want to talk about what you saw this afternoon."

"All right, go ahead," Jennifer snapped back. "You go first."

"I just hope that you're not going to tell anyone, that's all."

"You think I'd rat on you at school?" Jennifer asked. "You sure have a good opinion of me, don't you?"

"I don't care about school," Dawn said angrily. "I just don't want Mom to know because she'd tell Dad it was his fault for leaving and then he might not. . . ." Her voice stopped suddenly.

"I'm not going to tell anyone," Jennifer said. "I just wish you and Karla would stop, that's all."

"Karla told me she wanted to try new things," Dawn said. "She said she's sick and tired of being in a rut with the same boring people and the same boring things to do all the time."

Jennifer felt as if she'd been slapped. She

couldn't believe Karla would say that. But it was true. Karla was always wanting to do new and different things, like the photo contest. Is she really trying to say she's tired of being best friends with me? Jennifer wondered.

Suddenly Jennifer realized she was listening to the dial tone. She hadn't even heard when Dawn hung up.

Six

JENNIFER stopped going to Karla's locker and walking to homeroom with her. She seemed to be surrounded by Robbie and Dawn and Matt these days. Sometimes in homeroom though, when Jennifer accidentally glanced back at Karla, she'd find her staring back. But then she'd look away before Jennifer could smile or say hi or do anything at all.

Jennifer missed the telephone calls the most. Oh, sure, she missed walking to and from school with Karla and talking between classes at their lockers. But at school she had other kids to talk to. And Peter walked her home almost every day now.

But there was nothing to take the place of their phone calls. Karla used to call day or night with the zaniest things on her mind that she just had to say at that very minute.

Mrs. Barnes used to say that every time Karla saw a phone, she thought she was supposed to use it.

But Karla wasn't calling Jennifer anymore. She hadn't called in a week now. Probably Dawn's phone was ringing all the time though. Between Karla and the boys at school calling her, Dawn's phone must never be quiet.

Then Jennifer had a sudden thought. What about that guy she'd tried to call from here? Did he call her at home? Come to think of it, she'd seen Dawn coming from the pay phone outside the office at school a couple of times. Her eyes had been kind of watery and red then too. What was going on there?

Jennifer sighed. Saturday morning seemed long without Karla. They almost always spent Friday nights sleeping over and Saturday mornings were just a continuation of the talking and fun they'd had the night before.

But today would definitely not be like that.

Mom knocked on her bedroom door. "Mind if I come in?" her mother's voice asked.

"No, come on, Mom." Jennifer looked around her room and decided it wouldn't do any good to throw anything under the bed. Her mom probably knew what the mess looked like anyway. It hadn't changed since yesterday when she had brought the vacuum cleaner in. It was still standing in the middle of the room, waiting to be used.

"Thought I'd get my vacuum cleaner," Mrs. Barnes said, coming in and pointing it toward the door. "Unless you have plans."

"Nag, nag, nag," Jennifer said, trying to sound funny and light. She even tacked on a smile at the end of the last nag. But her mom read right though it.

"Why don't you call Karla?" Mrs. Barnes asked as she leaned against the vacuum cleaner.

"I did, last week," Jennifer began. "But the line was always busy."

"Are you sure?" Mrs. Barnes asked.

Jennifer picked at the fringe on her bedspread. "She's got other people to talk to now."

"Meaning Dawn?"

"Yes."

"But Dawn's your cousin. Why can't the three of you be friends?"

"I've just been eased out," Jennifer said.

"There must be some mistake." Now her mom sat down on the bed.

"Mom, I'd rather not talk about it, if you don't mind," Jennifer said. She jumped up and walked over to the window and looked outside. The last of the maple leaves skittered along the sidewalk.

"Tell you what," Mrs. Barnes began. "Why don't I invite Grace and Dawn and Karla and her mom . . ."

"No!" Jennifer shouted, turning around to face her mom. "No," she said again, softer this time. "I'm going to wash my hair."

She ran into the bathroom before she started to cry. She began to rummage around in the cabinet for her shampoo. When she couldn't find it, she looked in the shower. Then she remembered that she'd used the last of it the day before.

Oh, well, she thought, pulling on jeans and a turtleneck sweater. I'll go to the drug store and get another bottle. At least it gives me something to do.

Jennifer zipped her jacket up to her chin and walked quickly to the neighborhood drugstore. It was in a small shopping center only three blocks from the house. She and Karla used to go there when they didn't have time to go downtown.

Now Jennifer hurried past the ice cream store, the dry cleaners, the pizza parlor, came to the drugstore on the corner. She went inside and looked around. Not many people were there this morning. Good, she didn't feel like talking to anyone.

Jennifer walked down the aisle to the shampoos, rinses, gels, and all the other goo that people put on their hair. What had they done with her brand? The store always carried it. Maybe it was on the bottom shelf this week.

"Oh." Jennifer felt someone brush her back.

"Sorry, I didn't see you down there."

Jennifer glanced up. "Karla."

"Jen," Karla said, looking suddenly uncomfortable. "I didn't see, I mean I didn't know it was you." She looked away, then looked back again. "What are you doing down there?"

"Looking for my shampoo."

"Here it is." Karla grabbed a bottle and handed it to her. "Unless you've changed."

"I'm not the one who's changed," Jennifer shot back, hoping Karla got the message.

She did. "Jen, I know I haven't called. It's just that I've been so busy."

"I noticed." Oh, boy, Jennifer thought. I sound like a jealous character on one of those soaps Mom watches on TV. She began to examine her bottle of shampoo carefully, as if she'd never seen anything like it before. "I don't suppose you can come over or anything, can you?"

"When?" Karla asked.

"Now." Jennifer saw that Karla was wearing mascara this morning. That was a first.

"I can't. I'm getting ready to do something to my hair. It'll take all day."

"What?" Jennifer asked. "Your hair looks great the way it is."

"But Dawn said . . . ," Karla stopped.

"Go on. Tell me what my cousin said."

"She said it would photograph better if it was highlighted."

"You're not going to do that, are you?"

"No, Dawn is. She says that she's seen it done and knows just how to do it." As Karla ran a hand through her hair, Jennifer saw a flash of nail polish. Another first.

Suddenly Jennifer realized what Karla said about a photograph. "Are we still going to be in the Fashion Friend Photo Contest? We must not have much time left if we're going to enter our pictures. I know I didn't seem that thrilled about it at first, Karla. But now I think it's a really good idea."

"That's just it . . . " Karla's voice trailed off. "I've been going to tell you." She stopped again before going on. "Well, you didn't seem very interested and we could never get together to plan what we were going to wear for the picture, so . . . ."

"So what?" Jennifer didn't want to hear what Karla was going to say next. She already had an idea what it was. "So what are you trying to tell me?"

"Well, when I said something to Dawn about it . . . ."

"She said you two should do it together, since she's the expert and all."

"Well, she is," Karla said hotly. "And I thought you'd be happy that Dawn and I have teamed up. After all, you're the one who said we had to be friendly with her when she moved to town because she was so upset about what happened with her folks."

"I am, I mean, I think I am." Jennifer felt so confused now that she wondered if she'd ever get her feelings straightened out. Why did life have to get so complicated all of a sudden? "I think it's great that you and Dawn are having such fun together." Somewhere, deep inside her, she really meant those words. It just hurt so much to say them.

She put the bottle of shampoo back on the shelf and turned to walk away.

"Don't you want this?" Karla called after her.

"No." Jennifer shook her head, then left the store as quickly as she could. A light mist began to fall as she walked down the street. It was rapidly turning into a cold rain. Jennifer tucked herself into her jacket as far as she would go.

"Jennifer! Hey, Jennifer!"

From far away she heard her name being called, but she didn't bother to turn around. Jennifer felt awful, as if she were coming down with a strange disease and might never recover. Why did she have to feel so awful? Why couldn't she shed a friend the way a snake sheds a skin?

"Jennifer!"

Now the voice was right beside her. "Hi," she said from underneath her jacket. "Oh, it's you, Peter." She hadn't seen him since they'd gone to the Dairy Dream on Thursday afternoon. Was that a real date? She couldn't be sure. Only Dawn would know that. After all she was the expert.

"Yeah, it's only me. I've been to the library, researching my social studies report. Have you started yet?"

Jennifer tried to focus. "What social studies report?"

"The one that was assigned yesterday."

"But it's not due for two weeks."

"I figured I might as well get started." Peter grabbed her arm before she stepped in a puddle. "And besides, I didn't have anything else to do this morning."

That makes two of us, Jennifer thought. "What's your report going to be about?"

"The Gold Rush in California," Peter answered.

"Tell me what you've found out so far."

Jennifer looked at him and smiled. Amazingly, he wasn't blushing. He looked like a normal guy her own age, even kind of cute.

Before Peter could begin, the rain came down harder, pelting them with icy slivers.

"We're going to get drenched," Jennifer called. "Come on, I'll race you to my house for some hot chocolate."

"It's a deal," he said. They ran the rest of the way and Jennifer only pulled ahead of him when they charged up the front steps to the porch.

"I won, but I'll bet I looked like a drowned rat doing it," Jennifer said, shaking her dripping hair away from her face.

"Not to me you don't," Peter said.

Jennifer opened the door and led the way to the kitchen. Wow, she thought. I think he likes me. Wait till I tell Karla. Then she remembered. She wasn't going to call Karla ever again, about anything.

Seven

"SEE you tomorrow, Peter," Jennifer called before she closed the front door on Friday afternoon.

"Is that you, Jen?" her mom called from the kitchen.

"No, it's . . . it's . . . Martha Washington." She had decided to write her social studies report on presidents' wives.

"To what do I owe the pleasure of this visit?" her mom asked as Jennifer walked into the kitchen.

"I'm hungry." Jennifer opened the refrigerator door and stared inside. "Hey, what's going on? Are we having a party?"

"Don't touch the goodies. Your Aunt Grace and Dawn are coming over tonight."

Jennifer slammed the refrigerator door. "Oh, Mom, why?"

"Because they're our relatives, that's why."

Now Mom turned from her chopping board and the pile of celery pieces on it. "Honey, I talked to Grace this morning. She's terribly depressed so I invited them over. I invited that nice man up the street too."

"You mean Mr. Howell, whose wife died last year?"

"Yes, that's the one. He's lonely too."

"This is going to be interesting." Jennifer's first impulse was to reach for the telephone and discuss it with Karla. Then she remembered that she wasn't doing that any more. But she could just imagine what Karla would have to say. They could talk and talk for hours.

"Call Karla," her mom said. Now she was chopping onions and her eyes were watery.

"You just don't understand," Jennifer began.

"That's right," Mrs. Barnes replied. "I just don't understand why you and Karla don't just sit down and talk everything out."

"We tried, last Saturday at the drug store." Jennifer came over and watched her mom chop until her eyes began to water too. "What I found out is that Dawn's help in the photo contest means more to Karla than my friendship."

"That doesn't sound like Karla," Mom said.

"Don't be too quick to judge her."

Jennifer jumped as the telephone began to ring. "I'll get it upstairs, Mom," she said, hoping it might turn out to be Karla after all.

"Hello," Jennifer said breathlessly.

"Hi, Jen, it's Sue Beth. Got a minute?"

"Sure, what's up?" Jennifer wondered if she wanted to come over.

"Oh, nothing special." Sue Beth paused. "I just thought it would be fun to talk, that's all."

Jennifer waited, wondering what they should talk about. Not boys and not Dawn. "Have you started your social studies report yet?" Boring, Jennifer thought. Think of something else.

"I started it yesterday, at the library. I saw your cousin Dawn there," Sue Beth said. "She was coming out of a telephone booth by the front door and she didn't look too happy."

That guy, Jennifer thought. Why does she keep calling him? "Don't ask me to explain her, even if she is my cousin," Jennifer said.

"I don't know anybody who can," Sue Beth said. Then her voice sounded warmer. "Hey, I saw you at the library too. But you were too busy talking to notice."

Jennifer felt herself blushing. She was glad that Sue Beth couldn't see her face. She and Peter had gone to the library to work on their reports, but mostly they talked when they weren't being shushed by the librarian. Peter was the most interesting boy she'd ever known. She'd never realized that boys with brains could be so interesting. And he was kind of cute too.

"Peter just walks me home and stuff," Jennifer said.

"Have you had a date yet?" Sue Beth asked.

"I'm not sure what to call it." Jennifer didn't add that she'd been hoping that he might ask her to the Harvest Hop.

"That's great, Jen," Sue Beth said. "Really super. I wish . . ."

"What?" Jennifer asked, then realized what Sue Beth was thinking about. "Oh, Sue Beth, you've got to stop daydreaming about Matt. You'll find someone else."

"It's not easy to stop liking a person just because that person has stopped liking you."

Jennifer felt as if she'd been stung by a bee. That's just the way she felt about Karla. No wonder Sue Beth sounded so sad. Suddenly Jennifer felt she had to do something to make her feel better.

"Sue Beth, let's do something fun real soon."

"Like what?"

"Let's go roller skating. We'll get a bunch of

kids and go together."

"When?"

"How about next Wednesday afternoon?"

"Great. Who are we going to ask?"

"Boys. Lots and lots of boys," Jennifer said, laughing.

They started to make up a list of names to call and then divided the list in half. "I'll start right now," Sue Beth said. "I'll call Karla for you."

"And I'll call Matt," Jennifer added.

"Oh, Jen, this is going to be so much fun," Sue Beth said just before they hung up.

Aunt Grace and Dawn arrived a few minutes early and Mr. Howell knocked at the door right on the dot of six. Then Mr. Barnes introduced everyone and Mrs. Barnes served some funny-looking little things on bits of toast. Aunt Grace tried to talk to Mr. Howell. Jennifer thought they sounded as stiff as those people on foreign-language tapes that her mom listened to while she ironed. Finally Mr. Barnes started telling jokes and everyone laughed. That helped a lot. Jennifer didn't look at Dawn the whole time.

"Aunt Helen, will you excuse us now?" Dawn asked sweetly, a few minutes after everyone had finished Mrs. Barnes' apple and raisin pie for dessert.

"You girls run along," Mrs. Barnes said. "I'm sure you've got things to talk about."

"Like boys," Mr. Barnes said, winking at them. "Boys like Peter, for instance."

Oh, no, how did he find out? From her mom, probably. And now Dawn knew too. That meant good-bye, Peter, Jennifer thought. It's been good to know you.

Jennifer noticed that Dawn smiled the sweet, goey smile she reserved for grown-ups as they left the dining room.

"I've got to talk to you," Dawn said when they were upstairs in Jennifer's room. "But first, tell me about Peter. Is he your boyfriend now?"

Jennifer shrugged. "Maybe. What do you want to talk to me about?"

"Look, I know it may seem weird that Karla and I teamed up for the photo contest, especially after you two were going to do it," Dawn began. She paced back and forth from bed to dresser.

"Weird isn't the word," Jennifer said, straightening some papers on her messy desk.

"I was only trying to help Karla a little bit," Dawn said. "My dad said I should put my talent to work, helping others."

"Yeah, I saw what you did to her hair." The streaking made Karla look as if she'd combed

74

her hair with yellow paint.

"I never dreamed she'd ask me to take your place in the contest."

Jennifer glared up at Dawn. It was hard not to believe her when her eyes looked so innocent.

"You're not mad, are you?" Dawn asked.

"Try sad," Jennifer said. "That's what I am."

Dawn shrugged. "Well, as long as you're not mad. I can't stand it when people don't like me." She walked around the room, touching things on the dresser and looking at pictures of Jennifer's friends on the bulletin board. "Do you suppose I can make a telephone call in your folks' bedroom?"

"Go ahead," Jennifer said. All of Dawn's pacing and talking was suddenly making her nervous.

Jennifer thought about the phone call, wondering if it was to that older guy Dawn had met at the roller skating rink again. How many times had she talked to him anyway?

When Dawn came back a long time later, she looked as if she'd been crying. What's going on here? Jennifer wondered. But it was none of her business and she wasn't going to ask. There was no way she would get mixed up in any more of Dawn's secrets.

The next morning Sue Beth hurried up to Jennifer in the hall at school. "I called everyone on my list," she said. "How many did you talk to?"

"Not too many yet, but I'll finish calling after school." Then Jennifer went on to explain about Dawn and her mother coming to dinner last night.

"Did you call Karla?" Jennifer asked, trying to sound as if she didn't care.

"Yes, and she said she wouldn't be able to make it." Sue Beth touched Jennifer's arm. "I'm sorry, Jen, I really am. I know how you two have been best friends for so long. I don't know what's wrong with her."

"Don't worry about it," Jennifer said quickly. "I'm not." Jennifer didn't want Sue Beth to know she was telling a big fib so she turned quickly and walked into homeroom. Karla was already seated at her desk.

"Hi," she said. Karla's eyes brightened when she looked up and saw Jennifer.

"Hi," Jennifer answered, then sat down. She wished she could turn around and start talking, just the way she used to, about anything at all. It didn't matter what, as long as it was with Karla.

Jennifer felt a touch on her shoulder and looked up.

"I'm sorry I can't go skating on Wednesday," Karla began. "But that's the last day of the photo contest and I have to take our pictures to the department store."

"Oh, I see," Jennifer said through stiff lips.

"If the pictures don't get in before the deadline, we'll be disqualified."

"I suppose," Jennifer nodded.

"And you know how I am." Karla tried to laugh. "I'm always late with everything. Last-minute Karla, that's me."

"Good luck," Jennifer managed.

But Karla didn't move. "Jen . . . ."

"Yes?"

"I've been wondering about Dawn."

"What's the matter?"

"Is she in some kind of trouble?" Karla asked, her brown eyes cloudy with worry. "I feel like I should tell somebody about the phone calls she makes at our house."

"I don't know what's going on with her," Jennifer said. She wanted to say more, but she remembered her promise to Dawn. Her secret phone calls had to remain a secret, even to Karla. "Don't worry about Dawn, she can take care of herself."

"I think you're right." Karla smiled before she returned to her seat.

Jennifer smiled, too. Talking to Karla again

felt good. And there were so many things she had stored up to tell her. If they ever really started talking again, the way they used to, it would take them days and days to catch up. And maybe it would happen. Maybe . . . maybe.

Eight

ON Wednesday morning Jennifer hurried downstairs to breakfast. Her mom and dad were sitting at the table, but they had already finished eating. Usually her dad was on his way out the door when Jennifer came down. He liked to get to work earlier than everyone else, to organize his day he always said.

"Morning," Jennifer said. "Aren't you going to work today, Dad?"

"In a minute," he said. He arranged his knife and fork and spoon very carefully across his plate. "Sit down, honey. We want to talk to you."

"I don't have much time," Jennifer began, looking at her watch. "I was just going to eat my toast standing here."

"I'll drive you if it gets late," he answered.

Jennifer sat down next to her father

wondering what this was all about.

"It's . . . about Dawn," her mom began. Her dad straightened his knife and fork some more without speaking.

"What about her?" Jennifer asked, her heart pounding faster.

"Well . . . ," Still her dad hesitated. "Grace called me at work yesterday."

"At work?" Jennifer shouted. "Is Dawn sick?"

"No," her mom said. "It seems that you and Sue Beth are having a skating party today and you didn't invite Dawn. And it was Dawn's idea to have it, according to her."

"Oh, that." Jennifer broke her toast in little pieces. "Is that all?"

"Is that all?" Mrs. Barnes echoed. "Jennifer, where are your feelings?"

"I had a party for her." Jennifer pushed her plate of toast pieces away from her. "I introduced her to my friends and she walked to school with me until. . . ." She stopped before she said, "until she stole my best friend."

"Think how you'd feel if this were the other way around," Mr. Barnes went on. "How would you feel if you were left out?"

I have been, Jennifer thought to herself.

"Grace said Dawn came home from school on Monday crying because you hadn't asked her to the party." Mr. Barnes stood up to get the coffee pot.

"It isn't a party, not a real party." Jennifer brushed crumbs from her lap. "It's just a bunch of kids getting together and going skating. Anybody can come who wants to."

"Then why not make that clear to Dawn?" Mrs. Barnes said. "Why don't you tell her at school that you'd like to have her go with you? After all, she's the new girl in town and maybe she feels left out."

Jennifer wondered if she should tell her mom and dad about how Dawn moved right in on anything she wanted. Dawn never was left out if she didn't want to be. But somehow, Jennifer felt her folks wouldn't understand.

"I'll ask her." Jennifer stood up and carried her dish to the sink.

She saw Dawn right after homeroom period, walking down the hall on her way to math.

"I was kind of ticked off when I heard about the skating get-together," Dawn said, shaking her dark hair away from her face. "After all, it was my idea."

"Anybody can come," Jennifer said patiently. "We didn't mean to leave anyone out."

"I can expect this kind of treatment from Sue Beth because she's just jealous. But I knew you wouldn't feel that way." Dawn gave a little skip before she went on. "I'm glad that's settled. Are you going to the Harvest Hop?"

"I don't know," Jennifer said. "Are you?"

"I've been asked by several guys," she giggled. "I just can't make up my mind which one I want to go with."

"That's really tough," Jennifer answered. "I'll see you at the rink this afternoon."

On her way to social studies, Jennifer wondered which boys had asked Dawn to the big dance. Matt, for sure, and Robbie, probably. But Dawn said several guys had asked. Several was more than two, usually it meant three. So who was the third guy?

Oh, no, Peter was going to write an article about her for the newspaper. Maybe he'd already interviewed her and asked her to the dance at the same time. And maybe Dawn had decided it would be fun to go with a brain instead of an athlete like Matt or an all-around guy like Robbie. Fun, is that all Dawn ever thought of?

That afternoon after school Jennifer and Sue Beth rode down to the skating rink on the bus. Peter said he'd come later after he finished his work on the newspaper.

"Did you ask Matt to come?" Sue Beth asked Jennifer slowly.

"Yes, and he said he wasn't sure." Jennifer knew Sue Beth would hate to hear that. But she'd hate to hear that Dawn was coming even more.

"That's okay, that you had to ask Dawn, I mean," Sue Beth said. "In spite of everything, I think she's okay. Do you know something?" Sue Beth asked suddenly. "I feel kind of sorry for her."

"Sorry?" Jennifer said it so loud that a couple of other passengers on the bus turned around to look at them. "Sorry?"

"Yes." Sue Beth nodded. "She seems so desperate to be Miss Popularity, to have friends, that she'll do almost anything to get them."

Jennifer leaned back against the bus seat. Sue Beth was right. Dawn did seem desperate. It didn't make sense because she had everything going for her. Looks, talent, brains, personality—what more did a girl need?

Dawn was already skating with Robbie when Jennifer and Sue Beth walked in the door. Jennifer had to admit they looked good. They were skating in rhythm to a fast beat and took the corners in sweeping curves. More kids from their class drifted in to watch them.

"I don't see Matt anywhere," Sue Beth whispered. "I'll bet he isn't coming, especially if he knows Dawn can skate like that with Robbie."

He knows, Jennifer thought. He knows.

But Matt came anyway. He stood around for a while, with his hands in his pockets, watching the action on the rink. Jennifer and Sue Beth were skating with some of the other kids when they spotted him.

"Why don't you ask him to skate with you, Sue Beth?" Jennifer whispered as she slowed down next to her.

"I can't," Sue Beth said. "He'll say no and then I'll die."

"How do you know he'll say no?" Jennifer whirled around to skate backwards in front of Sue Beth. "Maybe he feels rotten because of what he did to you and now he's too embarrassed to ask."

"Do you think so?" Sue Beth glanced at Matt who was standing alone by the railing.

"Would I lie to you?" Jennifer asked, laughing and pulling Sue Beth with her to the exit.

Jennifer went back on the floor to skate, trying not to watch Sue Beth and Matt together. But it was hard. Each time she circled, she could see them standing there, talking.

At least they're talking, she thought. But one turn around the rink later, Jennifer couldn't see them anywhere. What had happened to them?

"Watch where you're going," someone said behind her.

Jennifer whirled around. "Peter," she yelled. "Where did you come from? I didn't see you come in."

"You were so busy watching Matt and Sue Beth that you wouldn't have noticed an elephant." Peter nearly tripped. "And that's how I feel too. Like an elephant on these dumb things."

"Here, let me give you another lesson," Jennifer said, grabbing his arm. "Hey, you know this is a first for me? I've never given a skating lesson to an elephant before." Then they skated together until the manager announced a ten-minute break.

Jennifer and Peter came off the floor and went over to a bench and sat down. "Boy, am I glad to be back on something solid instead of that skating floor," Peter said.

"You did act as if you were skating in outerspace," Jennifer said and ducked to avoid Peter's make-believe swing. Then she glanced up and saw Dawn and Robbie standing in front of them.

"Hi, Peter," Dawn said. "I just wanted to say how much I think your skating has improved. You're doing really well."

"Thanks, Dawn," he said. "By the way I've been meaning to ask if I could interview you for the newspaper some time."

He hasn't interviewed her yet, Jennifer thought. But he's going to. He could still ask her to the Hop.

"You want to interview me?" Dawn practically shrieked. "That is practically the neatest thing that's ever happened to me. When? And what do you want to talk about?"

"About your school in Chicago and how you were on TV and all that," Peter said.

"How about Friday afternoon?" Dawn asked, her blue eyes shining.

"I thought we were going to play miniature golf on Friday," Robbie said.

"Oh, Robbie, this is more important. We can go there some other time."

Robbie nodded, but Jennifer could tell by the look on his face that he wasn't very happy.

"Maybe we better make it next Monday then," Peter said.

"Okay, Monday, right after school," Dawn agreed. "We can go somewhere and have a root beer and talk and talk."

"How about Mr. Batten's room?" Peter asked. "He's the advisor for the newspaper."

"Well, at least we can meet there," Dawn

said, winking. "Come on, Robbie."

"Just a minute, Dawn," Robbie said. "I want to ask Jennifer something."

"Hurry up, then. I'm thirsty." Dawn tapped her skate impatiently.

"I was wondering where Karla is," Robbie said. "Is she coming today?"

"I could have told you that," Dawn answered. "We're in the Fashion Friend Photo Contest and she had to take our pictures to the department store. Today was the last day to get them in or we'd be disqualified."

Robbie swung around to look at Jennifer. "I thought you . . ."

"No, Dawn and Karla are doing it together," Jennifer said quickly.

"Oh." Robbie looked as if he was going to ask something else but couldn't form the words.

"Robbie, come on, I'm going to die of thirst." Dawn pulled on his arm. They rolled away on their skates then, heading for the refreshment counter.

"That should be an interesting interview," Jennifer said after a couple of seconds had passed. "I mean, Dawn has lots of interesting things to talk about."

"Yes, it should be pretty interesting, all right," Peter said. Then he changed the subject and Jennifer knew she shouldn't talk about it again. But she wanted to. Boy, how she wanted to.

Nine

JENNIFER walked slowly home from school on Monday afternoon. She dragged her feet through the leaves that had fallen to the sidewalk from the trees overhead. It had been a long time since she'd walked home alone from school. First, there had been Karla. For years and years there had been Karla, then Karla and Dawn, and then Peter. Finally, she had a boy to walk her home for a little while. After today and the interview, would Peter walk Dawn home?

Dawn's never alone, Jennifer thought, giving some leaves a vicious kick. She always has somebody.

Jennifer was amazed at her nasty feelings. Dawn is my cousin, she thought to herself. She's been through a bad time and so I'm supposed to be understanding, nice, and all that stuff.

So why isn't she supposed to be nice to me? Jennifer suddenly wondered. Why isn't nice something that works both ways?

"Jennifer, wait."

She turned around and saw Sue Beth running toward her. Her jacket was open and her scarf was flying behind her. And she was smiling a great big smile that Jennifer could have seen a mile away.

"Don't tell me, let me guess," Jennifer shouted as Sue Beth came nearer.

"Oh, Jennifer, it's true." As Sue Beth caught up to Jennifer, her breath came in raspy gulps. "He asked me after school today. I'm going to the Harvest Hop with Matt. Isn't that super?"

Sue Beth began to jump up and down and her books and purse went flying. For a moment Jennifer forgot her own fears about not being asked and just enjoyed Sue Beth's happiness.

Finally Sue Beth began to gather her books and Jennifer retrieved her purse from a pile of leaves. "So tell me, what happened?"

"First, he said he was sorry." Sue Beth stood up and brushed leaves from her purse. "Sorry that he kind of lost his head over Dawn. You know . . . ." Sue Beth sighed and glanced up into the bare trees. "It was just a momentary infatuation over the new girl in town. Actually, it reminded me of that soap Mom watches on TV. I saw it one day when I was sick. This exciting, desirable new woman moves to town, see, and . . . ."

"Sue Beth." Jennifer pulled her friend's scarf over her mouth to stop her from talking. "Tell me about you, not the soap."

"Well, there isn't much else to tell," Sue Beth said, her blue-green eyes shining. "Matt just came up to my locker after school and asked me if I'd go to the Hop the way we'd planned since seventh grade. He said that talking to me at the skating rink last week made him realize how much he missed me."

"That's great!" Jennifer sighed.

"And all because of you," Sue Beth said. "You made me go over and start talking to him again. He was embarrassed, just like you said."

Jennifer smiled at her friend. Then she turned and began to walk quickly down the street so Sue Beth wouldn't see the tears that formed in her eyes. Sue Beth followed along and they both scuffed their shoes among the leaves. Jennifer felt so happy for Sue Beth, yet was overcome by feelings of sadness. Being thirteen could really be confusing sometimes.

"I don't suppose you saw Dawn or anybody

else, did you?" she said finally.

"Anybody else? You mean Karla?"

"I was thinking of . . . ." Jennifer paused. She didn't want to say that she was worried about Peter being the next one to be caught in Dawn's little web. Now that Dawn had let Matt go, she would probably replace him with someone else.

"You mean Peter, don't you?" Sue Beth asked. "No, I didn't see him, but don't worry. He'll ask you to the dance."

"It's okay if he doesn't." Jennifer tried to convince herself of that. "After all, I hadn't planned to go in the first place, remember?"

"I remember," Sue Beth nodded. "Only Karla and I were planning on it."

"She's popular," Jennifer said. "If Robbie doesn't ask her, someone else will."

"But she only wants to go with Robbie," Sue Beth reminded her.

"I know," Jennifer nodded. And now I want to go too and I only want to go with Peter, she thought.

"Here's where I turn," Sue Beth called out, stopping at the corner. "Call me if anything happens."

Jennifer turned down Pine Street, wondering what route Karla walked home these days. Jennifer never saw her coming down Pine

Street so she must be walking three blocks out her way on Elm.

I wonder how long it takes to get over losing a best friend, Jennifer thought, walking up the steps to her house. Is it like getting over the chicken pox or a bad sunburn or what? Maybe it's something that never goes away, she decided, as she opened the front door and went inside. Maybe it's like that scar I have on my knee when I stumbled on a rock. Maybe I'll have it with me the rest of my life.

"Is that you, Jen?" Mrs. Barnes called from the kitchen.

"No, it's . . . it's . . . ," Jennifer paused. She just didn't feel like being clever or funny today. "Yes, it's me."

Her mom appeared in the open doorway. "Good," she said. "I want to talk to you." Mrs. Barnes sounded furious.

Jennifer followed her mom into the kitchen. "What about?" No sense beating around the bush when her mom sounded that way.

"This." Mrs. Barnes picked up an envelope from the kitchen table.

"What is it?" Jennifer didn't want to touch it, afraid of what might be inside.

"Go ahead, it's already open."

Jennifer pulled the telephone bill out of its envelope. "What's this got to do with me? I only call Karla and I don't call her much any more. Besides, those calls don't cost extra."

"But there are a number of long distance telephone calls on the bill that I can't account for," Mrs. Barnes said. "Some were made from here and others were made from someplace else and billed to our number. Do you know anything about them?"

"Not me." Jennifer put the statement on the table. "I haven't called anyone."

"I didn't mean to accuse you, honey." Her mom's tone of voice softened. "What about Dawn? Does she ever use the telephone while she's here?"

"Sure, but she calls . . . ." Jennifer stopped. What was she going to do? Tell her mom about that older guy Dawn had met? After she promised she'd never tell?

"Jennifer, this isn't a time to keep a confidence because I think we must know what's going on."

"She isn't calling anyone long distance," Jennifer said. "She met some high school kid at the skating rink and she calls him when she comes over here. She doesn't want her mom to know."

Mrs. Barnes looked at the telephone bill again. "Have you ever heard her talking to this high school boy?"

"No." Jennifer shook her head, remembering. "No."

"I think I know who this is, but I'll call Grace to make sure."

"Is it someone in Chicago?" Jennifer asked. "Maybe Dawn has an old boyfriend in Chicago."

"These calls aren't to Chicago." Her mom paused. "I think this is a west coast area code. Let me talk to Grace first, will you, Jen?"

Jennifer walked slowly upstairs to her room. Who was Dawn calling anyway? Maybe she was just having fun. Maybe she just dialed numbers at random, talking to anyone who answered.

No, that wasn't it, Jennifer thought after a moment, remembering the last time when Dawn's eyes had been red from crying. She wouldn't have been crying is she'd been calling for fun.

The telephone rang and Jennifer hurried into the hall to answer it. Was it Peter? Jennifer's inside churned crazily. Suddenly she wondered if she really wanted to know.

"Hello." Her voice sounded weird, as if a parrot was doing a bad imitation of her.

"Jennifer, what's the matter?"

"Karla, it's you."

"I don't blame you for sounding disappointed,"

Karla said. "I'd be disappointed too, after what I've done to you."

"Oh, Karla, it's not that, well, yes it is too." Jennifer knew she sounded confused, but her thoughts were spinning around and around in her head. "No, I was trying to say I was expecting someone else's voice, that's all."

"I'll only take a second," Karla began. "It's just that I wanted to tell you something before I lost my nerve."

"Oh, no, take all the time you want," Jennifer began, then remembered her mom wanted to call Aunt Grace. "Except make it quick because Mom has to use the telephone. You'll never guess what's happened but I'm not supposed to say anything."

"Oh, can't you tell me?" Karla begged. "We never keep anything from each other, remember?"

"I remember," Jennifer said, wanting to laugh and cry at the same time. "But I can't talk. I mean, I can't use the telephone. Can you come over?"

"Oh, do you want me to?" Now Karla was screaming at the top of her voice. Dawn was right about one thing. Karla didn't need a telephone, not with lungs like that.

"I'll meet you," Jennifer yelled. "Start right now. Go down to Elm, over to Pine, the way we always walk."

But Jennifer was listening to the dial tone. Karla had already hung up. "I'll be right back," she yelled to her mom, grabbing her jacket and running out the front door.

She ran as fast as she could, flying down the street. Somehow she and Karla would straighten out their misunderstanding and then everything would be the way it always had been. Well, maybe not everything right away, but soon. They'd been such good friends once, they'd be best friends again in no time.

Jennifer saw Karla turn the corner at Elm. They came together in the middle of the block and threw their arms around each other, jumping up and down at the same time.

"I was so afraid you'd never speak to me again after what I did to you," Karla said when they finally stopped jumping and began talking.

"I'm okay," Jennifer said. "And I have to admit now that I wasn't really all that interested in the photo contest. I really hope you and Dawn win."

"But that's what I want to tell you," Karla said. "We haven't entered the contest after all."

"What? But you said you had to take the entry to the store last Wednesday. That's why you couldn't go skating with us."

"On the way to the store I started thinking," Karla said. "And I decided I'd rather throw away the pictures instead of my friendship with you."

Jennifer stopped. "But didn't the pictures cost you money and everything?"

"Mom took them so I only have to pay for one roll of film and the developing charge."

They walked on while Jennifer tried to sort it all out. "Dawn's going to be mad," she said, grinning.

"She already is," Karla answered. "I told her at school this morning and at first she was really steamed. Then she said she probably wouldn't have time to be in the contest anyway, since she was going to be busy after school from now on."

"Doing what?" Jennifer asked.

"She said she'd be writing for the newspaper," Karla answered. "Has she said anything about it to you?"

"No." Jennifer felt as if her insides had turned to ice. Newspaper writing meant only one thing. Dawn had decided to go after Peter.

"What's the matter, Jen?" Karla asked softly.

"Nothing."

"Come on, this is Karla talking. Your best

friend, remember?"

Jennifer smiled. It sure sounded great to hear that. She had a best friend again. If only she had a boyfriend. Well, win some, lose some, she thought.

Ten

KARLA listened carefully to Jennifer as they walked to school together the next morning. Jennifer told her everything about Peter. She told her how she'd first thought he was a brain and a nerd besides, but he wasn't a nerd at all. He was a brain, only the nicest brain she'd ever met, even if he did skate like an elephant. And he was cute, too. Not a dreamboat, but she'd settle for cute.

"But now you think Dawn has her clutches on him and so he's lost forever," Karla finished. "The way Robbie is lost forever, too. I don't know how she does it."

"I don't know about Robbie." Jennifer looked at Karla as they walked. "But Peter didn't call last night. I thought he might after the interview to tell me how it went."

"Maybe it was just ordinary," Karla said, pushing her curly brown hair away from her face. "Maybe there wasn't anything special to talk about."

"No." Jennifer shook her head. With Dawn as the subject, there was always plenty to talk about. Like the telephone call that came from Aunt Grace while she and her mom and dad were eating dinner. Jennifer knew that conversation had been about Dawn. But her dad wasn't telling and neither was her mom. What was going on?

"I know what," Karla said, shifting her books to her other arm. "If we don't get asked to the Hop, let's have a movie party at my house. My folks just bought a VCR. We can even have popcorn and put real butter on it, not that fake stuff they give you in the theater."

"Okay," Jennifer said. "Maybe my folks will give me some money and we can have a double feature."

"Maybe that will be more fun than going to the Hop." Karla tried to sound cheerful, but she didn't look it and Jennifer knew why. Karla wanted to go to the dance as much as she did. There was one thing that best friends couldn't replace now that they were thirteen, going on fourteen. That one thing was boys.

"Who are we kidding?" Jennifer asked. "This is awful. I thought it would be fun to have a boyfriend."

"At least we have each other," Karla sighed.

As they reached the front door of the school, they saw Dawn stomping toward them.

"Jennifer," she said her eyes blazing. "May I speak to you . . . ?" She turned and looked pointedly at Karla. ". . . alone."

Karla shrugged her shoulders. "See you in homeroom Jennifer," she said walking through the school's doors and down the hall.

"A fine cousin you turned out to be," she said to Jennifer after Karla left. "You're nothing but a snitch."

"You mean about the telephone calls?" Jennifer felt her face get hot. "Yes, I told and I'm sorry I had to break my promise. But Mom had to know and besides, you didn't tell me you had a boyfriend who lived out of town."

"Oh, Jennifer, you're just hopeless." Dawn flipped her dark hair away from her shoulders. "You can't get anything right." She turned and stalked through the door and down the hall.

What did I do? Jennifer wondered. I wasn't the one who made long distance phone calls to some high school guy and charged them to someone else. Dawn said she'd met the guy at the roller rink, but Mom said the area code was from the west coast. Could it be that Dawn was calling someone else? She stared after

Dawn as she felt a tap on her shoulder. She had to talk over this idea, but who . . . Someone tapped again, harder this time.

"Karla," she said as she whirled around. And then she felt warm and excited and dizzy at the same time. "Peter, I didn't hear you."

"I noticed," he said. "I wanted to tell you about the newspaper interview before you heard it from someone else." He glanced in the direction Dawn had taken.

"She didn't mention it," Jennifer said, waiting impatiently. "She was steamed about something else."

"By the way, I tried to call you last night, but you line was busy for a long time. I guess you and Karla are talking."

Jennifer laughed and then Peter did too. "Yes, but we weren't on the phone. Dad was talking . . . ." Suddenly she stopped. Yes, it was all making sense now. Dawn's phone calls and her red, teary eyes. . . .

"It's almost time for the late bell," Jennifer said. "I'd better get to homeroom."

"I'll walk that way with you," Peter said. "I wanted to tell you that the interview with Dawn went really well."

Jennifer's heart sank into her shoes. Now Peter was under Dawn's spell. She'd told him about her interesting life in Chicago, being on

TV, meeting a couple of rock stars, modeling clothes, and other things that Jennifer couldn't remember now. How could she compete with a girl like that?

"I'll use some of it in the paper," Peter began. "But I wanted you to know that I'll leave out the parts she made up."

"Made up?" Jennifer couldn't believe it. "What did she make up? And how do you know?"

"When she told me about meeting those rock stars, it got me thinking," Peter began. "I remembered other stuff she said to impress me, like writing a teen column for the *Chicago Tribune*. We take the Trib and I've never seen any columns written by her. I'd remember that. And when I started thinking about some of the other stuff she was dumping on me, like her dad being a movie producer out in Hollywood."

"She said that?" Jennifer couldn't believe it.

Peter nodded. "I plan to be a journalist one day, Jennifer, so I'm really careful about the stories I write. Dawn ought to be more careful too, about the stories she tells. You could drive a tractor through some of the holes in them."

Jennifer turned her eyes away from Peter. Poor Dawn, she thought. Why did she have to tell such lies to get attention? Was that the only way she felt important?

"And there's something else. . . . " Peter went on.

"I don't want to hear anything else about Dawn." Jennifer shook her head. She felt terrible.

"It's about the Harvest Hop."

Oh, no, she thought. Here goes. After Dawn lied, he still wants . . . .

"Will you go with me, Jennifer?"

Jennifer stared at him. "Peter, I . . . I . . . ," she began, stumbling and stuttering over the words in her mouth. She'd waited so long to be asked, and now she couldn't say yes.

"Don't tell me you already have a date," Peter said quietly.

"Yes," Jennifer yelled, finally getting the word out. "I mean no, I don't have a date and yes, I want to go with you." She was acting so nerdy, but she didn't care. She was going to the Hop with Peter!

"Terrific," Peter said, grinning. "I was afraid you'd want to go with someone else."

"That's funny," Jennifer said, but she wasn't laughing. "That's what I was afraid of too. That you'd want to go with someone else."

Peter stared hard for a moment, then slowly his smile disappeared. "Dawn? No way. Sorry,

Jen, I know she's your cousin, but I don't feel anything for her but sorry. Poor kid, she must have problems at home."

* * * * *

Later that night, when Jennifer was in bed, she thought more about Peter's words. Dawn must have problems at home, he'd said. And that was it, all right. Dawn's problem was no home, not a real home right now. She and Aunt Grace were living in a furnished apartment, no not living, just staying there until they decided where they were going to live. And Dawn's dad was somewhere in California, a long distance away.

Suddenly it came to Jennifer. Dawn had been calling her dad. Dawn's tears, her red eyes, Dawn wouldn't let a mere boy be that important to her. But her dad was important. And so was her mom. She must feel torn in half.

That wasn't a happy thought to fall asleep on, but a few minutes later, Jennifer did anyway.

When she awakened the next morning, Jennifer heard voices downstairs in the front hall. She ran to open her bedroom door.

"And that's what I've decided to do," Aunt

Grace said. "Finally, I've made up my mind about something."

"Are you sure?" she heard her dad ask.

"I'm sure." And Aunt Grace really sounded as if she meant it, Jennifer thought. Then the front door opened and closed and she knew Aunt Grace had gone.

Jennifer grabbed her bathrobe and slung it over her shoulders before bolting downstairs to the kitchen.

Her dad was staring into a cup of coffee and her mom stared out the window.

"I heard Aunt Grace," Jennifer began. "What's going on? Can you tell me?"

Mom and Dad looked at one another, the way they always did before they told her something important.

"Dawn is going to California to live with her father." Her mom's voice was soft and low.

"And Grace is moving back to Chicago. She got her old job back." Her dad's voice was quiet too.

"Dawn, moving to California?" Jennifer repeated as if she hadn't heard right. "Why?"

"Dawn needs . . . needs more discipline right now," her dad began. "Grace feels she hasn't been strong enough with her and Dawn definitely needs someone stronger, so they're going to try this for a while. Dawn has been a handful, I guess."

"I guess," Jennifer echoed. "I hope she'll be happy out there." As she said it, Jennifer realized she truly meant it. She really wanted Dawn to be happy.

"Dad, do you think they'll ever get back together, as a family?"

Dad shrugged. "We can always hope," he said.

"Then that's what I'll hope for," Jennifer answered. "I think Dawn has really missed what she used to have."

Finally the night of the Hop came. Jennifer had been so preoccupied with Dawn that she'd hardly had time to get nervous. But now, getting ready with Karla and Sue Beth in her bedroom, she felt all tingly inside.

"Jen, you look great in that dress," Karla said, squinting her eyes while she put on her mascara.

Jennifer looked down at the blue silky fabric of her dress. Then she looked at herself in the mirror. She had to admit, she didn't look half-bad. But she felt so nervous inside that she thought she might blow up!

"Help, you guys," Sue Beth yelled from the bathroom door. She came out with lipstick smeared above her lips. "The guys will be here any minute!"

Jennifer and Karla both looked at her and laughed good-naturedly.

"It's times like this that we could really use Dawn's help," Karla said, reaching for a tissue and dabbing at Sue Beth's lips.

"Yeah, why'd she move to California anyway? I thought she and Aunt Grace were from Chicago," Sue Beth said, between Karla's dabbing.

Jennifer sighed. "She moved out there to live with her dad." She left out the part about Dawn calling him long distance, begging him to come home. Aunt Grace had explained that Dawn thought it was her fault that her dad had left.

But Jennifer didn't need to have anyone explain the rest. Dawn had been so desperate for everyone to like her that she'd try anything, even lying, to win a friendship.

Poor Dawn, Jennifer thought. She just didn't understand that to have friends, you have to be one first.

The doorbell rang, interrupting her thoughts. Suddenly, her stomach started doing flip-flops. She took several deep breaths to calm her nerves. Then she checked herself in the mirror one last time. She turned to Karla and Sue Beth and smiled her best smile.

"Come on," she said. "Let's go find the guys."

About the Author

ANNE HARLER has written 40 books for young people and more than 100 articles and short stories for adults' and children's magazines. She has also written and produced many radio and television programs for children.

Anne was born in Galesburg, Illinois. Galesburg is the hometown of Carl Sandburg. Anne read many of Sandburg's books at an early age.

"Students growing up there inherited a literary legacy," she has said. "That early influence gave me the hope that I, too, could become a writer one day. Fortunately, that's all I've ever done and I couldn't have wished for more."

When she is not writing, Anne enjoys traveling with her husband to far off places. She also enjoys backpacking California's High Sierra, reading history and biography, tap dancing, and practicing magic.

Anne and her husband have lived in San Marino, California for many years. They are the parents of four grown children.